W9-BLI-736

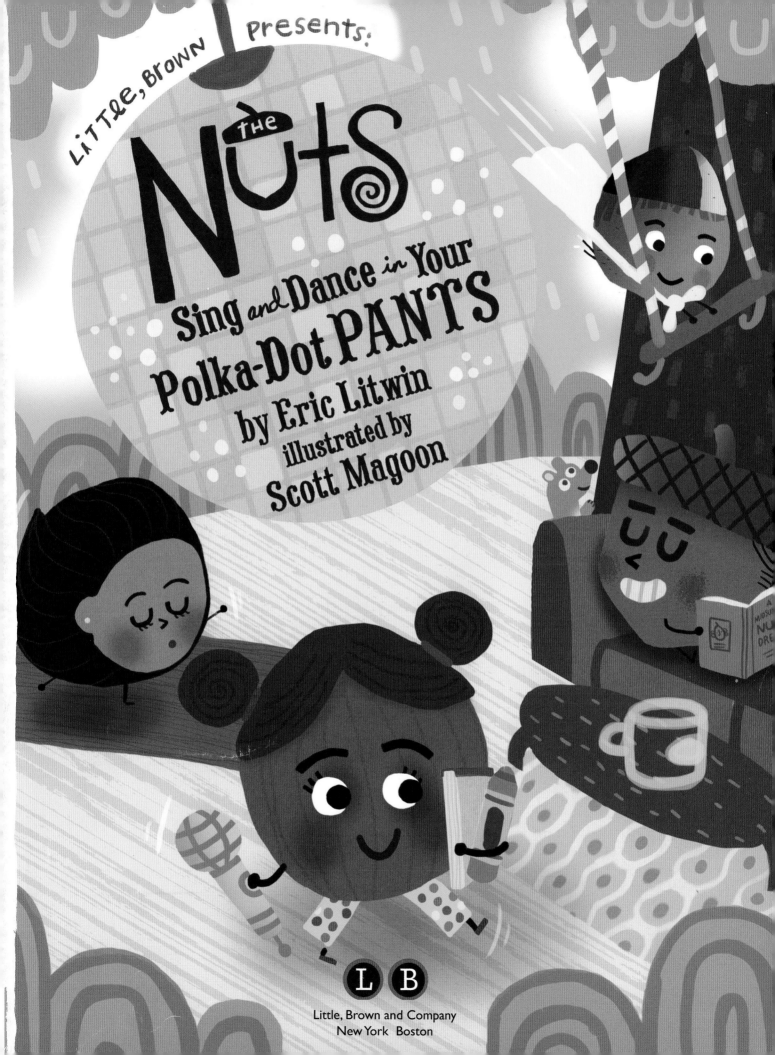

Hazel loved to sing and dance.
Hazel loved her polka-dot pants.

Polka-dot pants.

Polka-dot pants.

Sing and dance
in your
polka-dot pants.

Oh, No!

Papa's nose
was stuck in a book.
He didn't see Hazel.
He didn't even look.

WOULD PAPA DANCE?
NOT A CHANCE.

But Hazel kept rocking
in her polka-dot pants.

Polka-dot pants.

Polka-dot pants.

Sing and dance
in your
polka-dot pants.

Oh, No!

Mama Nut
was crazy busy.
She ran up and down
in a dizzy tizzy.

WOULD MAMA SING?
NOT A CHANCE.
WOULD PAPA DANCE?
NOT A CHANCE.

But Hazel kept rocking
in her polka-dot pants.

Polka-dot pants.

Polka-dot pants.

Sing and dance
in your
polka-dot pants.

Oh, No!

Her little brother,
Wally Nut,
was being a pain
in the you-know-what.

WOULD WALLY PLAY?
NOT A CHANCE.
WOULD MAMA SING?
NOT A CHANCE.
WOULD PAPA DANCE?
NOT A CHANCE.

But Hazel kept rocking
in her polka-dot pants.

Oh, No!

Hazel Nut rocked all alone.

So Hazel Nut picked up the phone.

Hazel knew just what to say.

WHO DID HAZEL CALL THAT DAY?

GRANDMA NUT
burst through the door.
She disco-danced
across the floor.
She said, "Grandma loves you
through and through,

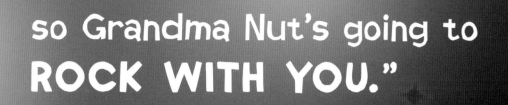

so Grandma Nut's going to
ROCK WITH YOU."

Polka-dot pants.

Polka-dot pants.

Sing and dance
in your polka-dot pants.

Oh,
Yes!

Mama, Papa, and Wally, too,
heard that happy hullabaloo.

The next thing they knew
they were tapping their feet.

Their heads began bopping
to the bop-able beat.

They started to sing.
They got up to dance.
And that family rocked together
in their polka-dot pants.

GO TO THENUTFAMILY.COM TO HEAR THE WHOLE SONG AND SING AND DANCE ALONG WITH ERIC LITWIN!

DO THE POLKA-DOT PANTS DANCE!

Polka-dot do-do-do.

Polka-dot pants, polka-dot pants.

Polka-dot do-do-do.

Polka-dot pants dance!

Go up,  go down,

go up, go round and round.

Go this way, go that way,

go this way, go every way!

To the front, to the back,

to the front,

and then clap clap clap!

**Download free songs
and dance along
at TheNutFamily.com!**

To the Fantastically Fun Fishman Family —EL

For everyone out on this dance floor—keep bustin'! —SM

About This Book

This book was edited by Allison Moore and Liza Baker, and designed by Kristina Iulo with art direction by Saho Fujii.
The production was supervised by Erika Schwartz, and the production editor was Annie McDonnell. The digital illustrations were created using Adobe Photoshop and a very nutty imagination. The book was printed on 128gsm Gold Sun matte paper.
The text and display type were set in Skizzors, and the jacket was hand-lettered by the illustrator.

Text copyright © 2015 by Eric Litwin
Illustrations copyright © 2015 by Scott Magoon
Cover art © 2015 by Scott Magoon
Cover design by Kristina Iulo
Cover © 2015 Hachette Book Group, Inc.
Music produced by Michael Levine

All rights reserved. In accordance with the U.S. Copyright Act of 1976, the scanning, uploading, and electronic sharing of any part of this book without the permission of the publisher is unlawful piracy and theft of the author's intellectual property. If you would like to use material from the book (other than for review purposes), prior written permission must be obtained by contacting the publisher at permissions@hbgusa.com. Thank you for your support of the author's rights.

Little, Brown and Company

Hachette Book Group
1290 Avenue of the Americas, New York, NY 10104
Visit us at lb-kids.com

Little, Brown and Company is a division of Hachette Book Group, Inc.
The Little, Brown name and logo are trademarks of Hachette Book Group, Inc.

The publisher is not responsible for websites (or their content) that are not owned by the publisher.

First Edition: September 2015
Library of Congress Cataloging-in-Publication Data
Litwin, Eric.
The Nuts : sing and dance in your polka-dot pants / by Eric Litwin ; illustrated by Scott Magoon. — First edition.
pages cm
At head of title: Little, Brown presents.
Summary: Hazel Nut wants to sing and dance, but Mama, Papa, and Wally Nut are too busy, so Hazel calls in a special family member to get everyone moving.
ISBN 978-0-316-32250-8 (hardcover) — ISBN 978-0-316-29981-7 (ebook) [1. Stories in rhyme. 2. Dance—Fiction. 3. Singing—Fiction. 4. Play—Fiction. 5. Nuts—Fiction.
6. Family life—Fiction.] I. Magoon, Scott, illustrator. II. Title. III. Title: Sing and dance in your polka-dot pants.
PZ8.3.L7387Nw 2015
[E]—dc23
2014043318

10 9 8 7 6 5 4 3 2 1
APS
PRINTED IN CHINA